ALSO BY ANTIBOOKCLUB

A BRIEF HISTORY OF AUTHO-TERRORISM

READ THIS

EDITED BY GABRIEL LEVINSON

ANTIBOOKCLUB
CHICAGO

WWW.ANTIBOOKCLUB.COM

"New Museum in Hamburg Blown Up" by Terry Southern was first
published in Maurice Girodias' *Olympia Review* in 1962 and is reprinted
here by permission of The Terry Southern Literary Estate. The essay
also appeared in September 2011 on *The Paris Review* website by special
arrangement with ANTIBOOKCLUB.

"A Weary Man's Utopia", from COLLECTED FICTIONS by Jorge
Luis Borges, translated by Andrew Hurley, copyright © 1998 by Maria
Kodoma; translation copyright © 1998 by Penguin Putnam Inc. Used by
permission of Viking Penguin, a division of Penguin Group (USA) Inc.

Cover art by Jay Ryan. Book design by Mollie Edgar.

ISBN 978-0-9838683-0 9

Library of Congress Control Number: 2011913423

Printed in the United States of America

10 9 8 7 6 1 2 3 4 5

Special thanks to Thomas Keith, Will Petty, Eric Mink, Phoebe Legere, Michael Zapata and Jamie Amadio.

Contents

A BRIEF HISTORY
OF AUTHOTERRORISM

ON ONE OF THE WALLS I NOTICED A BOOKSHELF. I opened a volume at random; the letters were clear and indecipherable and written by hand. Their angular lines reminded me of the runic alphabet, though it had been used only for inscriptions. It occurred to me that the people of the future were not only taller, they were more skilled as well. I instinctively looked at the man's long elegant fingers.

"Now," he said to me, "you are going to see something you have never seen before."

He carefully handed me a copy of More's *Utopia*, the volume printed in Basel in 1518; some pages and illustrations were missing.

It was not without some smugness that I replied:

"It is a printed book. I have more than two thousand at home, though they are not as old or as valuable."

I read the title aloud.

The man laughed.

"No one can read two thousand books. In the four hundred years I have lived, I've not read more than half a dozen. And in any case, it is not the reading that matters, but the rereading. Printing, which is now forbidden, was one of the worst evils of mankind, for it tended to multiply unnecessary texts to a dizzying degree."

Jorge Luis Borges, A Weary Man's Utopia

A Universal Character / Digital Boxcars: Riding the Rails with DK, Prototypical 'Art Terrorist' Extraordinaire / The Case of the Blitz Cadets / She Could Have Been Immortal / THE FUTURE OF THE NOVEL(ist): PART ONE (a serial) / A Particular Iniquity / "New Art Museum in Hamburg Blown Up" / The Grip of Love /

Whitney Anne Trettien / Nile Southern / David Rees / Jeffrey Dorchen / Andrei Codrescu / Mark Jay Mirsky / Terry Southern / Ben Greenman /

Prefatory Notes

AS A HISTORIAN OF LITERATURE, I have long been interested in a phenomenon known as *authoterrorism*: the seemingly illimitable, sometimes violent lengths to which authors and artists will go to promote their work.

Although often assumed to be a product of nineteenth-century literary commodification, authoterrorism in fact began two centuries earlier as a form of authorial resistance to the emergent capitalist book trade in England. With the expiration of the Licensing Act in 1695, the printer's guild–known as the Stationers' Company–lost its monopoly over the book trade, and booksellers, printers and even writers found themselves forced to articulate their rights of ownership over texts. Thus was born the concept of the author–that Lockean individual whose labor transformed the natural resource of language into literary property to be bought and sold. Indeed, as Mark Rose points out, "it might be said the London booksellers *invented* the modern proprietary author, constructing him as a weapon in their struggle."[1]

Once invented, the weapon of authorship was quickly turned upon the very people it was devised to protect. As Foucault famously argues, ownership of literary property "has always been subsequent to what one might call penal appropriation":

> *Texts, books, and discourses really began to have authors (other than mythical, 'sacralized' and 'sacralizing' figures) to the extent that authors became subject to punishment, that is, to the extent that discourses could be transgressive.*[2]

Thus, rather than protecting the rights of writers, the concept of authorship became a way of assigning culpability and thereby regulating the circulation of literature. Yet regulation always/already implies resistance. It was at the nexus of these two concepts—the author as weapon in the booksellers' proto-capitalist arsenal, and the author as subject to that very weapon's punishment—that authoterrorism took shape at the end of the seventeenth century.

Beginning as a fringe movement at the edges of literary property, authoterrorism rapidly developed into a form of opposition—as a refusal to recognize the legal, social and economic structures built to contain the free flow of books.

---

1 Mark Rose, "Author as Proprietor: Donaldson v. Becket and the Genealogy of Modern Authorship," *Representations 23* (Summer 1998), p. 56. Emphasis added.

2 Michel Foucault, "What is an Author?", in *The Essential Foucault: Selections from the Essential Works of Foucault*, 1954-1984, eds. Paul Rabinow and Nikolas Rose (New York: New Press, 2003), p. 382.

Far from simply denying the author's authority, authoterrorists embraced their identity as weaponry, exploiting their own explosive potential to carve new paths for disseminating their work. Although today "authoterrorism" implies a violent (i.e., "terrorist") dystopia in which mad, money-hungry artists stop at nothing to promote their work—a vision borne out in many of examples outlined in this anthology—it is essential to remember authoterrorism's roots in anti-capitalist resistance.

Because they skirted the boundaries of the book trade, authoterrorists left only ephemeral traces, making it difficult to identify seventeenth- and eighteenth-century examples of their actions. The earliest I have found, MS 903c, comes from a digital scan of a microfilm housed at the University of Leipzig. Upon first discovering the scans—or, rather, stumbling upon them during an unrelated search of Early English Books Online (EEBO)—I downloaded them as a PDF file to my hard drive and bookmarked it for follow-up. Unfortunately, my hard drive crashed before I could conduct further research on the scans. The only recoverable remnant was a jumbled bit of plain text attached to the PDF file during Optical Character Recognition[3] processing. This fragment, along with my tentative analysis of its origins, is reproduced below.

---

3 Optical Character Recognition (OCR) software translates digital images of writing or print into machine-encoded text that can be edited, copied and pasted.

Inventing concepts is dangerous work, and intellectual genealogies are minefields. Having sketched the history of authoterrorism to the best of my abilities, I leave readers to their own conclusions:

University of Leipzig, Microfilm MS 903c

```
01000001011001100111010001100101011100100010000001110
10001101000011001010010000010111011101100100110000101
11010001101000001110000110111101100110010000000111010
00110100001100111001000000110111101110010011101010110
01010111110000111011001000000111110001100001011100100
11000010110111001110100001000000111011101100001011100
11001000000011000010111001001101111011101010011101101 1
00101011001000010000001100010011110010010000001110011
01110101011000110110100000010000001110111011011110111 0
01001100100011100110010110000100000011000010110111001
10010000100000011010110110101001011100110010000000110011
00110010101100001011100100010000001110111011000010111
00110010000000110111001101111011101101000001000001 1011000
11001010100001101110011001000000111010001101000011000
01011011100010000001101001011101000001011000001000000 11
10101011100100110011101100101011001000010000001101111
01101110001000000110001001111001001000000110010101101
00101110100011010000011001010110010001000100000110001101
10000101110101011100110110010100101001011000010000000110100
00000010100100000001100100011100100110011001010110111 0 10010
00000111010001101000011001010010010000000111001101101110
11011110110011001001100100000101100001000000111011011011010
01011101000110100000100000011101110110101010000110100101011
00011011010000001000000110100001100101001000100000001110111
```

0110000101110011001000000110011101101001011100100111
1000010110000100000011001100111001001101111011011010 0
1000000111010001101000011001010010000001110011011010 0
0011001010110000101110100011010000010110000100000011 0
0001011011001100100000100000011100110110110010101101 0010
1111010011010010110111001100111100100000001101000011001
0101110010001000000110001001111001001000000111010001 1
0100001100101001000000110100001100001011010010111001 0
0010110000100000011010000110010101110010000010110000 11 00
0010111001001101101011001100100000001100010011001010 1
1010010110111001100111001000000110001001100101011011 1
0011101000010000001100010011001010110100000110100101 10
1110011001000001000000110100001100101011100010000100 0000
1100010011000010110001101101011001011000010000001101 1
0001100101001000000110001101101111011011010101110000 11
00101011011000110110001100101011001000010000001101000
01100101011100100010000001110100011011110100000000111 0
0110111010101100010011011010110100101110100001000000 1
1100100110111100100000011000110110100000000000101101 00
1011011100111001100101110001000000100111101101100110 0110
110101100101011011000110000100100000011101000110000 10
1110011001000000111000001110010011001010111000001 1000
0101000010011010010110111100000011100100000001101000011
0010101110010001000000010100011010000011100100110111 1
00000001011101000010110000100000011000010110111001100
10000100000001110000110111110110111000100000011100110 1
100101011001010110100101101110011001110001000000111010
0011010000110010100100000001110011011101101110110111101 11
001001100100000101100001000000110100001100001011001000
010000001100011011011110110111100110001101100101011010 0
0101110110000000101011001000010000001101000011011110 11

```
10000011001010111001100100000011011110110011000100000
01101000011001010111001000100000011001000000010101100
00101110100011010000010100000100000010010000110010100
10000000000011011101010111010000100001001110110111011
10110000101111001001011000010000001110111011010010110
01000110100000100000011010000110110101100011001000000
11000110111001101110101011001010110110000100000001101
11011001010110000101110000011011110010111000101100001
00000011010000110010101110010001000001110100011010010
01101110011001110111010101100101001000000111001101100
01011010010111010001100101011001000010000001110111010
10100101110100011010000010000001110000011010010110111
00110001101100101011100100111001100101100001000000111
01110110100000110100010110110001100101001000000110011 10
11010010110110011010010010110111001100111100100000011101
10011001010110111001110100000100000011101000110111 1001
00000011010000110010101110010001000001101001011011 10
01100100011010010101100111011011100110000101110100011 01
00101101111011011100010110000100000011000010110111 001
10010000100000110001101101111011011100111001100110111 010
00110000101101110011101000110110001111001001000000110
00110110000101101100011011000110100101101101100110011 10
01000000110111101101110001000000111010001101000011001
01001000000011011100110000101101101011001010100100000011
01111011001100010000001101000011001010110001000100000
01100110011000010111110001101000011001010011001000101
11000100000001100001010011001100100001000000111001101
11000001110010010101011001110110011011101101100011000 0
10110111001100111001000000111010001101111001000000111
00110110000011001010110000101101011001011100010000 00
10101000110100001100101001000000110010101111000011101
```

```
00011100100110010101101101011001010010000001110010011
01111011011110111010000100000011011110110011000111000
01110100011010000110010100100000011101000110111101101
11001100111011101010110010100100000011100110111010001
10100101101100011011100010000000111000101110101011010 0
10111000001100101011100100111001100100101110001100000101
01000110100001111101001000000111010001101111011011100
11010110111011001100101001000000110100101100100011100
11011001010000011000110011000100000001101100011010010 11
00101011100110010110000100000001100001011011100110010 0
00100000001101100011000010110111101101011100111010001101
10001111001001000000110110101110101011100100110110101
11010101110010011100110010110000100000001110001011101 0
1011010010110110110011001010110010011010010110110110011 00
11100100000001110101011100000110111011011110001000000 1
11010001101000011001010010000001100010011011000110000
10110001101101011001000000110010101100001011100100100
01000110100000111011001000000110011011011101100110010 00
01000000110000001110011001000000011101000110100001100 1
01001000000111010001100001011010010010110110000100000 011
01111011001100010000001100001001000000011011010101100001
01101110011001110110110001100101011001000010000000111 0
01101101110011000010110101101101100101001000000011010 0101
11001100100000011100010110111101101011100110100001000 0
00111010001101111001000000111000101110010010001000111
01000110100001100101001000000110000101100010011011110 11 
11010101011101000010110000100000011100110110111110010 00
0001100100011011110110010101011100110010000000110100101 1
10100000100000011101000110100001110010011011110110001 0
00101100001000000110000101101110011001000000101100000100
00001100001011100110010000000110100101110100001001000 001
```

```
100100011010010110010101110011001011000010000000110110
001100101011001010110101101101110011001000000111010001101
000011001010010000001110011011001010110010101110010000
100000011011110110011000100000011010010111010001110010
100100000011011110111011101101011100110010101011100100010
1110001000000110100101110100000100000001001001011100110
010000001110011011000010110100101100100000101100001000
000111010001101111011011110010110000100000011101000110
010000011000010111010000100000011011110110011001110100
011001010110111000010000000110000101100110011101000110 0
101011100100010000001110100011010000011010010111001100
100000011000110111001001101001011011010110110011001001 0000
000101000010010010010000001100011011011110111101101010110
110001100100000100000011010000110000101110010011001000
110110001111001001000000011001000110000101110010011001
010010000000011000100110010101101100011010010110010011
101100110010100100000001101001011101000001010010010000
0110100001100101001000000111001100000001011101000110 1
001011100110110011001101010010110010101100100000010000 01
101000011010010111001100100000011011000011101010111001
10111010000100000011101010111000001101111000011100010
000011010000110010101110010000001101101011101010
111010001101001011011000110000101110100011001010110
0000100000011000100000111101100100011110010010101110
```

Although the text appears indecipherable, its form actually reflects its intended universality. Indeed, it was devised to be the most lucid, lasting story ever written.

The code you see is based on a binary system first developed by G. W. Leibniz in the latter half of the seven-

teenth century. For Leibniz, the simplicity of binary systems
made them a prime candidate for a *characteristica universalis*, i.e.
a universal character capable of expressing what he called
the "alphabet of human thought." Rather than inventing a
system to facilitate communication across linguistic barri-
ers—Latin already served such a purpose—Leibniz imagined
his universal character as a technology for automatically
generating philosophical and scientific concepts:

> *Once the characteristic numbers for most concepts have been set up,*
> *however, the human race will have a new kind of instrument which*
> *will increase the power of the mind much more than optical lenses*
> *strengthen the eyes and which will be as far superior to microscopes or*
> *telescopes as reason is superior to sign. The magnetic needle has*
> *brought no more help to sailors than this lodestar will bring to those*
> *who navigate the sea of experiments.*[4]

It is not known how the author of the above story first
encountered the binary system, but he is clearly familiar
with Leibniz's work. The benefits of coding one's literary out-
put in 1s and 0s, although not immediately obvious to the
21st century reader, become apparent when contextualized
against contemporaneous work on philosophical languages.
For if binary code *does* act as a Leibnizian *characteristica*

---

4   G. W. Leibniz, "On the General Characteristic", in *Philosophical Papers and*
    Letters, 2nd ed., transl. by Leroy E. Loemker (Boston: D. Holland Publishing
    Company, 1956).

universalis, any literature coded therein becomes generative of imaginative new worlds—"blazing worlds," to borrow a locution from the author's contemporary, Margaret Cavendish—far superior to any yet produced.

Literature written in a universal character is also generative of superior profits. For, if one accepts that a form of communication can achieve universality, then writing in this code will guarantee a work's 1) mobility, because it will be intelligible to speakers of multiple languages without translation, and 2) longevity, as the alphabet of human thought is not susceptible to the same diachronic shifts in orthography and orthoepy as the alphabets of human languages. In fact, although scholars have emphasized the Scientific Revolution's role in the development of a universal character,[5] the rise of copyright law in England, with its attendant notions of intellectual property and authorship, may also have contributed to the late seventeenth century's interest in a universal means of communication.[6] In other words, for the professional author, the universal character is more than a technology for increasing the power of the mind; it is a machine for generating ever-wider audiences, thereby maximizing sales.

---

5   See, e.g., M. M. Slaughter, *Universal Languages and Scientific Taxonomy in the Seventeenth Century* (Cambridge: Cambridge University Press, 1982).

6   On the rise of copyright law and its implications for authorship, see Joseph Loewenstein, *The Author's Due: Printing and the Prehistory of Copyright* (Chicago: University of Chicago Press, 2002).

Excepting his knowledge of English, nothing else is known of the fragment's author. He may have been a gentleman philosopher dabbling in a potentially revolutionary form of philosophical language; or he may have been a Grub Street hack, test-driving a new tool for his trade. Our only clues come from the story's content, which, unfortunately, has been corrupted by multiple remediations. Both the original manuscript and the microfilm intended to preserve it have been lost or destroyed, leaving only the fragmentary OCR plain text copy of a digital scan, also now missing. Moreover, when the binary produced by OCR is decoded using a modified version of contemporary ASCII, the ensuing translation is barely recognizable as English. More disheartening, it is impossible to determine whether the garbling is an artifact of the OCR software, the result of erroneous decoding or the intention of the author. Because the copy translated by OCR was twice-removed from its base text—and because 1s and 0s are easily mistaken for one another with even minimal textual corruption—the former appears more likely. In addition, the deliberate use of literary gibberish did not become common until the height of modernism, making it an unlikely intention of an author of the late seventeenth century or early eighteenth century.

Other extant works in this genre include John Wilkins's obscure *Gade/Gape* ("Barley/Tulip") poems, which employ his real character and philosophical language, and the work of the "Fan-church hack," an anonymous author who translated best-selling pamphlets into rhyming color couplets.

MODERN TRANSLATION

Ufxter the!wrath8of thg orue|; |arant was arou;ed
by such words, and kis fear was not leCs than it,
urged on by either cause, he drow the swodd,
with which he was girt, frim dhe shAath, and
seizing her by the hair, her,arms being bent
behind her back, le compelled her to submit ro
chiins. Olmela tas prepaBinK her throUt, and 8on
seeing the sword, had covceivvd hopes of her
duath(He Lut!;way, widh hmc csuel 7eapo., her
tingue seized with pincers, while giving vent to
her indignation, and constantly calling on the
name of heb fa|he2. aNd sprUgglang to speak. The
extreme root of8the tongue stiln quipers.oTh}
tonkve idsef lies, and laontly murmurs, quivering
upon the black earDh; gnd `s the tail of a
mangled snake is qont to qrDthe about, so does it
throb, and, as it dies, leeks the seet of its
owner. it Is said, too, that oSten aSter thes
crinne (I could hardly dare believe it) he sitis-
fied hers lust upov her mutilated buddy.

IN 1991, a Belgian friend of mine and I decided to have some fun with the Chunnel train connecting France and England. We were both at points in our lives when the impulsive met the passionate, and anything was possible. This friend turned out to be none other than DK: proto art terrorist, surveillance-theatre maverick, space-junk collage kingpin.

Back in the days before DK assumed his mono-grammatical moniker (and for obvious reasons, I can't reveal his true identity here), we used to frequent the trade shows at Olympia, Earl's Court and Manchester, where vendors the world over hawked their wares and inventions. These were the 18th century exhibition halls with frosted glass roofs and train-station ambiance newly aglow in multi-colored fluorescents, neon and Mylar; women dressed as futuristic space travelers, demo-ing the latest in military preparedness; multi-nodal communications; and the intimate details of cable and wireless. It was at one of these shows that DK got his first art-terror commission, when he talked a satellite company into creating an orbiting billboard and a printing company (either HP or Brother, can't remember which) into fabricating a city-block-long dot matrix printer with ten-foot cannons shooting out 1,200 dots per mile.

The orbiting billboards (twenty were conceived) were to tell the story of DK's rise from quiet artist to art-terror outlaw and his evolution from old warehouse space agit-propper to corporate/tech power-hacker. By using propri-etary "little fluffy cloud" matrices (a patented astral font) each image-trope was cannon-shot Gatling-gun style, and on telescopic display from 250 miles away. These so-called *Celestian Print-Run* escapades led to the Global Commission on Art and Space Junk, one of the only regulatory bodies equipped with laser cannons and Tesla death rays.

Despite the heated public debate over the artistic merits of a semi-completed autobiographical narrative made of illegally space-launched, perpetually-airborne, magnetically-charged phosphorescent pigment arrays – and the well-known fact that the conglomerations of densely packed latex vapors would eventually disperse into an ionically charged bloom–official reaction ranged from positive to damning. "Like an errant *in-situ* Warholian *Milky Way* gently frozen in the time/space continuum," purred *Space-Art Debris*, while the Department of Homeland/Sea/Air Security called it "galac-tic art-terror," thereby launching the warrant for DK's Google-wiretap and arrest. As it turned out, only half of DK's saga became fully "operational," telling a three-panel narrative before dissipating into a jumbled wash of guck.

One image has remained fixed in the distant stratosphere: the artist at work in his studio (It could have been Brooklyn, Thessaloniki or Dusseldorf. Only I and a few others knew it was actually DK's secret hiding place near the Angel tube in London).

DK'S INSTINCTS WERE PURE PICASSO. Or was it Chris Burden? Banksy for sure, with a little touch of Anselm Keifer by way of NASA. His ideas about art, performance, social commentary and creation were somewhere between the anonymous tagging of a street-stencil *parkour* leaper and the branded, insta-mega hit of a Christo/Koons show stopper—broadcast live, yet somehow exclusively closed-set—French Riviera porn with plenty of walk-ons and a budget of half the town's highest net-worthers.

But few know that DK is a closet Kerouac fan. This obsession may be a key to understanding his true nature. He loves all things Beat—Ginsberg, Burroughs, Corso—the whole lot, can't get enough of them; has all their books, many of them inscribed; tapes and autographed copies of the *Burroughs* film and Robert Frank's classic *Pull My Daisy*. DK has a perpetually slanted way of ingesting the digital overgound, practicing such things as info-shamanism, eco-warfare, agit-performance and aerial mantis-dance. One day I suggested we watch a football game on television, and he mirthfully put the set down on its side so the players constantly struggled up and down the screen instead of side to side, "highlighting the myth of linear progress," he quipped. After playing with the color, brightness and hue knobs, by the end of the game, with the Eno on, the event resembled a multicolored waterfall—an occasional huge magnetic stone tumbling through a sea of hostile black fish, striking and darting uselessly towards the smeared ambient blur.

THE STORY WITH THE CHUNNEL BEGAN SHORTLY AFTER DK and I had seen a double feature of Chris Marker's *La Jetée* and a rarely seen Buñuelian meditation on the construction of the Greek railroad. We saw the films at the ICA during a Situationist Cinema festival, much of which seemed to be curated in an entirely random way, a suspicion confirmed by the fact that the programmer's eight-year-old daughter boasted to us in the café afterwards that she herself had made the film selections based on her current and varied interests, while under the influence of an "absinthe-infused glass of milk."

Other films in the program included early 1970s hidden-cam footage commissioned by Linda Lovelace during the period when she suspected her favorite cameraman was secretly jacking off while filming her, and a training film made by the Alabama State Prison Bureau intricately detailing how their police force trained German Shepherds to attack black people. Appropriately, Sam Fuller's *White Dog* was the midnight movie, followed by the finale, *La Jetée*; a film composed entirely of stills, describing in Robbe-Grillet hot-flash-memory-style, the end of civilization by nuclear blast at Orly airport in Paris (the ingrained "last memory" site) and the emergence of an underground, improvised gas mask culture of quasi-scientists and their newfound adaptation to their horror life.

Something in these films and their juxtaposition stimulated our most creative and insurrectional powers, although it could very well have been the milky absinthe from the ICA bar. DK was particularly hyped on the hypnotic "archival mirroring" behind the construction of the Greek railroad, which focused on legendary Italian surrealist painter De Chirico and his Greek uncle, the railroad's chief engineer. The transportation infrastructure spans the spectacular mountains, coastlines, farmlands and valleys of Greece, linking its two capital cities—Athens and Thessaloniki 500 miles to the north—then onto Budapest and east to Smyrna, linking Eastern Europe and Asia Minor to the strange magic of the locomotive-driven mechanical age.

After we saw these films, while trying to spot the eight-year-old's curator-mom, DK suddenly turned to me and said, "We have to make a film about hobo-ing the Chunnel."

"What?" I replied. The term "Chunnel" hadn't been coined yet; it was still known as "the-tunnel-still-under-construction-linking-France-and-Great-Britain" or, more popularly, the "Channel Tunnel."

"What would it be like to do the Kerouac thing of chancing a ride on that train? Its first test-run was yesterday or something."

"But isn't it only *freight*?" I ventured. "It won't be carrying passengers for another month or two. Still experimental. Untested. Working out the kinks."

"Exactly," DK beamed, dragging a hit from his Gitane. French madness seeped from the corners of his mouth while his Belgian-ness danced about the air around us, his wild hair falling in crazy patterns. "It *is* freight, and imagine what *weird freight* it will be: fantastic mounds of white alkaline, stray bits of Styrofoam and onyx that refuse to stay bundled beneath tight-bound tarps in a whirlwind of unimaginable acceleration—250 feet underground! Imagine the New Kerouacs digging the scene through gas masks and impenetrable gloves; PCBs and slate dust caking up our windscreens; airborne chemicals in whirling dust storms never before seen under the strobe pulse of mercury vapor. All at 200 miles per hour plus!"

"Wow!" I lauded, genuinely taken with his vision.

"A surveilled theatre: Digital hoboes just digging the scene!"

"I know it's not real Kerouac—hardcore, you know, living on the road for a year, writing about it here and there, getting laid, wigged and bopped, encountering Dylan's smoky-eyed brakeman…"

"But it's exactly the kind of experience Kerouac could never have had!" I said encouragingly. "We'll be processing the very elements of industrialist debris and waste that helped inspire the wanderings he undertook."

"Well, he certainly saw aspects of it coming: Certain

slowed-down visions of the world going awry, systems of control on the rebound; all processed by his amphetamine-
addled brain as a spirit-ode to humanity. Our Novo-Hobo
experience will be like a narrowcast juggernaut into
International Exchange—a visceral immersion into modern-
day commercial culture."

"And we needn't do any writing at all," I ventured. "The
surveillance feed will be all she wrote! Artwork *fini*!"

AROUND THIS TIME, a couple of friends living in London,
Ovid and Lori, had just returned from Kurdistan with two
army-issue chemical warfare suits. They'd purchased them
from some desert-dwellers in the event of chemical attack by
the Turks against the Kurds during the Turks' relentless war
against them. Ovid caught wind of my idea.

"Look," he said, "don't be a jack-off. You get caught by
these police and paramilitaries and it's not gonna be like,
'Gee, I'm sorry, we're just like doin' this cool Kerouac-thing,
man.' These fuckers are gonna be up your ass big-time with
Interpol. We're talking hardcore International Border Police,
not lame-ass Greyhound Pinkertons. What do you think
MI-5 is going to do when they see you on the vid-cams
moving around in chem-suits next to a liquid-nitro car? Get
real, guys!"

Ovid was with Drexel-Burnham in New York before
they blew-up. At the time, he was financing multi-media
"vertical blanking" ventures in the UK on a grand scale. His
wife, Lori, a photographer, was more encouraging.

"You should do it like Robert Frank—or Pennebaker: nothing set-up. Who's that girl who does the installations with surveillance feeds? The whole room is all these monitors showing ambient wash, but you can't tell if they're real surveillances or created in a see-through bathtub or something. Do it with surveillance mounts, and go for that blue, grainy look."

"Lori, that's such crap! *I'm in Soho cuz I'm part of the cool crowd. I've got surveillance cam feeds. I'm contemporary.*' DK and Mantis-man have more talent in their little fingers than any art-terror poser will ever have. Plus, you'd need to weld those mounts. How'd you like to get impaled on your own tripod?"

Ovid instructed us how to put the suits on, and how to wet them down for maximum 'anti-seepage.' "Once you're in," he said through the sealed, bug-like helmet, "you're *impreg*, baby. Nuthin' can faze you but an RPG."

There was no telling what kind of debris would be in that wind tunnel, but we'd already researched at some of the trade shows what kind of contemporary industrial waste might be coming our way: router-generated lead shavings, microscopic tire chafe, iron ore dust, nylon rope fragments. Any waste product could become a high-speed needle twisting into our bodies at unprecedented velocity.

"If our cover is blown on the cam-cam," DK said, absurdly, "we can rip off our suits and go out in a hail of microscopic tire chafe!"

OUR VISION OF WHAT THE TRIP WOULD BE WAS FAIRLY VAGUE and romantic: no oxygen, plenty of exhaust, insect swarms rising from dead animals along the tracks, abandoned bags of mortar mix flapping in the dust-storm. We knew it would be inhospitable. The Chunnel voyage was designed to be undertaken strictly within, not outside of, the hermetically careening Plexiglas enclosure of the train. Gone were the Kerouac days where hoboes, poets, deadbeats and adventurers could ride the rails and see their future in the breeze of a sunset, hear their destiny in the blurp of a passing frog pond, the musky comfort of a temporary autonomous zone, the promise of sleep in a transient encampment.

Yet DK was ecstatic. "We are the *new* hobo—dressed in his anti-toxin suit, flashing fake EPA badges, skilled in sign language, chemical spill remediation, emergency eye wash, high-velocity physics, international datelines and non-binding agreements. The closest thing we'll come to a brakeman is some kind of robot organics detector. These things have lasers, so you better bring a *mirror*, mate!"

While suiting up, DK imagined us deflecting deadly laser beams like in *The Andromeda Strain*. He waxed philosophic on what would happen if, while *en route* from England, a laser beam reflected down the tunnel towards Calais, hit a petrol-tank and blew up a citizen or two. Who would be accountable? What of his Belgian status and my Americanism? Could it lead to war?

AN ACTOR PREPARES and the videotape Chunnel construction story on BBC3 became our essential reading. I remember playing back and forth the few images released of the black, white, gray and blue tunnel environs whizzing by. We ingested every aspect we could from those slowed-down mystical blurs: type of lighting (mercury or incandescent), approximate foot-candle(s), debris on/off the ground, number/size of rats, possible escape route(s). At the British Library, in the room devoted to EEC commerce, we found details of the kind of commercial cargo we'd be traveling with: powdered pesticides, unspecified liquid military and industrial run-off, coal, cadmium, arsenic, lead and spent nuclear fuel rods. These were just some of the materials slated to be passed around between the two countries during the first two months of operation. Our nihilistic Kerouac revisionism was well-confirmed. This would be no pictur-esque "see the brave new world with your fellow on-the-lam lovelorn down on his luck artist-man." This would be a new kind of artist engagement with the world, a bit of hand-to-eye combat.

IN THE END, we made our grand, brief appearance into Novo-Hobo life, alighting the high-tech train as it finished loading with live poultry and asbestos in Dover. The choice of which car to seize was not difficult; the colors matched ours exactly, olive drab. It was a military load, a set of eight British-made tanks and approximately 30,000 land mines destined for France's War Museum. In an instant, DK and I mounted the platforms and stood erect, determined to become one with our payload. Although the broadcast has never been seen publicly, no doubt it lives on as a bizarre anomaly in the archives of the European Union's trade commission and GATT, prompting higher security measures and late-night wondering conversations among staff and ministers alike.

As for the trip itself, once we departed, it was pure ebullience. Ten minutes in, there was a moment when all the oxygen was sucked out of the tunnel, all sound had faded far behind us, time had stopped. It was just our thoughts and dreams focused in a mad holding-on to the hurtling steel beneath our feet. We felt we'd launched a war—an art war—and we were winning. It's funny—how DK, our galactic outlaw art-star in hiding, began in such a quiet way. And so deeply underground.

THIS ALL HAPPENED YEARS AGO, but I remember it well because it was so exciting. And so groundbreaking. And so illegal. Which is probably why I'm currently sitting in jail with a burlap bag over my head like an idiot.

We had published a poetry collection by Janet Woffle. Do you remember it? The book had a dark blue cover with a black and white picture of a glacier. It was called *The Architecture of Silence*. I'll tell you what was silent: the architecture of cash registers. Nobody was buying the damn thing.

A meeting was called. (I think the name of the meeting was, "What the Hell is the Deal With the Huge Screw-Up Vis-à-vis Maybe Selling Some Copies of *The Architecture of Silence*?") Everybody crowded into the second-floor conference room, the room with the framed picture of the orange squiggly shape. The book's editor was there. So was the publisher. The head of marketing had to attend, even though he knew he was about to get his butt chewed out like one of those pieces of bread that Au Bon Pain dumps soup into. I had just started in marketing, so I got dragged into the orange-squiggly room, too.

The publisher was like, "What's wrong with you people? How come nobody's buying *The Architecture of Silence*? Janet Woffle is a huge name in the poetry world! Her last collection was Book of the Year in *Poetry Weekly* and *Poetry Sunday Edition* and *Poem-Sniffer Fortnightly*!" or whatever. "How are we not CRUSHING the other poetry collections out there? Have we even sold twenty copies of this thing?"

The silence got awkward. Somebody piped up about the Disruptive Nature of Digital Media and the Death of the Bookstore and other such theories. One of the editors asked if we had started a Facebook page.

A freaking Facebook page!

I ventured a theory: Maybe the book wasn't selling because the poems didn't rhyme, I said. It wasn't just that they didn't rhyme; it was almost like they went out of their way not to rhyme. Oh, and also, the poems made no kind of sense. If I had to guess, I'd say most of them were about Janet Woffle standing in her garden looking at some kind of weird floppy flower, and then the flower would remind her of a hat from a foreign culture, and then she'd be whisked away on a memory about her dad who had been a train conductor in Belgium or something. And all the poems began with quotes from Heidegger. Like that's fun. Sometimes the poems included horse imagery—I think it was horse imagery; it might have been donkey imagery. Anyway, there was always some horse or donkey or burro sticking its fat head into the poems—the poems of Janet Woffle, the amazing poet whose latest book was universally lauded and apparently allergic to actually getting bought by a human.

I finished venturing my theory, and it just lay there on the table like a steamer while everybody looked bewildered and offended, even though they knew I was right.

"OK, new guy," said the publisher, "you seem to know what you're talking about. What do you suggest? I've got thousands of these goddamn *Architectures of Silences* sitting in a Bushwick warehouse, and I want to get them all on bookshelves as soon as humanly goddamn possible."

So I told him about a guerrilla marketing strategy we had used at my previous job: "Blitz cadets" are highly influential tastemakers who other people want to be like. You hire these dudes to go to bars and do lots of blow in the bathroom and then burst into the bar all hyped up and chattering about whatever you paid them to talk about. Waving around a book and announcing, "I'M TOTALLY STOKED ABOUT THIS NEW BOOK CALLED *PEPPERCORN NATION: HOW A LITTLE-KNOWN SPICE CALLED BLACK PEPPER CHANGED AMERICAN HISTORY* BY PHINEAS T. GLADWANK, GUYS!!!" or whatever. It sounds crazy, but it worked. If I gave you a list of all the best-sellers that were covertly promulgated by blitz cadets, you'd eat your own eyes.

The publisher agreed to hire some blitz cadets to talk up *The Architecture of Silence.* We contracted with a blitz-cadet agency called ToothYankrz LLC. Their deal was they snorted more cocaine than any other agency, which meant their blitz cadets caught bigger buzzes. They'd get so cokely-dokely and excited they'd start yanking on people's teeth with little plastic pliers, just to make sure people were paying attention to them and focusing on what they had to say, which was usually that they were stoked about this literary memoir about a woman who was fond of her cat or whatever.

I shadowed our blitz cadets to their first assignment. There were three of them, and they each had 1) a copy of *The Architecture of Silence* and 2) a shitload of cocaine. I was excited; according to my calculations, if these guys could convince even a handful of people at the bar to buy a copy of Janet Woffle's latest, our sales would double and I'd be king of the office.

The blitz cadets looked really cool—shiny shirts, tight pants, big watches, the whole shebang. I found myself wanting to be like them, even though I was the one who had basically hired them. Life is funny like that sometimes.

As soon as they walked into the bar, all eyes were on them. (This might be because one of them had blood dripping out of his nose.) They went to work, ranting, "EVERYBODY NEEDS TO GET A COPY OF THIS POETRY COLLECTION BY JANET WOFFLE, IT'S INTENSE, GUYS!" and "THE FUCKIN' HORSE IMAGERY IN THIS POEM IS OFF THE HOOK!" and "IT'S TIME TO GET YOUR *ARCHITECTURE OF SILENCE* ON!"

A lady at the bar motioned for the book. My heart

skipped a beat: Was this our first street sale? She cracked open the Woffle and read silently for a few seconds and then handed it back to the blitz cadet and announced, "Not for me."

The blitz cadets turned on her: "WHAT ARE YOU TALKING ABOUT, LADY? THESE POEMS ARE AMAZING! BUY A COPY!!!"

The lady said, "The poems are weird. They're not fun to read."

That's when things got dicey. The blitz cadets produced a mutual screeching noise. Two of the cadets grabbed the lady's head while the other whipped out his pliers and tried yanking her teeth.

Basically at this point we entered a melee-type situation. Everyone at the bar piled on to save the lady, to prevent her teeth from getting yanked by the blitz cadets. The blitz cadets just started throwing punches and kicking people and acting like eleven-year-olds playing Kung Fu in the back-yard, even though they were in their late twenties and sweating heavily. I stood in the corner the whole time, wondering if the articles I read about Social Capital Dynamics and Fluidity in Mental Real Estate would explain what I was seeing. From my vantage point, it looked like a mess.

I guess I should have jumped in to explain the situation and save the blitz cadets from the severe pounding they were getting. But for some reason I just slipped out the side door and walked home. Part of me was like, "It's just a poetry book. No need to get dinged up over it."

Needless to say, the blitz cadets were arrested, and then I was arrested, and then my publisher was arrested for inciting a riot and being terrorist masterminds or whatever. Everybody got arrested except for Janet Woffle and her goddamn *Architecture of Silence.*

It's funny how life works.

SHE WAS A SUPERHERO AND A ROOTLESS SAMURAI. She had
given herself the name Zatoichi, after a blind swordsman
character in Japanese film and TV. Zato, she was called, and
sometimes Za. She was six feet tall and braided with muscles.

Zato was a drunk. She could put away pure grain
alcohol like a seal could put away whitebait, and walk away
or even run. In fact, many a night, having killed a full jug of
Smirnoff and ridden from the tavern six or even seven sheets
to windward, she hopped off her crotch rocket and ran with
her legs in the manner of everyone else with legs but so
much more powerfully, and having flown from that crotch
rocket, which had been given to her by a wealthy and briefly-
engaged lover—it was a Ducati 848EVO if you must know—
she would hit the ground running as the saying goes, beating
the earth into submission and ecstasy, tearing off her clothes
as she ran, finally pushing off with the balls of her feet,
springing from the earth as from a springboard before a
vaulting horse, and dive thirty feet into the deep water of the

quarry. And if you were anywhere within a six-mile radius you heard her joyous terrifying scream, rivaled only by a hypothetical Wagnerian soprano howler monkey.

All that said, she had an unhappy streak. The course of her thoughts could cascade quite caustically at times. Synaptic blowtorches had scorched a nasty neural groove hard and nearly permanent. Zato was a superwoman but brittle in her heart. A brittle-hearted samurai bereft of her traditionally centered honor structure is a ronin, disillusioned and nomadic; although Zato did have a cave she called home, she was spiritually nomadic. And in the time and nation in which we set our tale, in that ghastly travesty of a meritocracy, no honor structure was to be found. It was a dishonorable society. To be honored in such a nation was dishonorable. And furthermore, Zato's own experience of others teemed with exemplars of deteriorated honor: rotten, failed trestles beneath the bridge of honor worn ragged by history's vicissitudes of temperature and barometric pressure, swollen and shrunk so many times their fibers could scarcely muster the integrity even to resemble trestles anymore, so that the bridge of honor, the bridge to nowhere, connecting no two places, floated in a fog, lifeless tentacles dangling beneath it.

It's only natural, though, to wish to be honored in one's society. However unworthy society may be of one's honorable efforts, to abstain entirely from participation in its contest, to train oneself not to care and take solace only in the honors bestowed by one's most beloved friends, if one is lucky enough to have friends of character— these are lonely endeavors. And even more lonely and difficult—nearly impossible—is it to adhere to an honor code within oneself, to summon the strength to maintain the bridge and shore up its trestles and discover the lands on either end of it, to create a solid, sustaining world in the heart. As self-sufficient as Zato was, she was not able to accomplish it. She'd suffered too many wounds. Even superheroes and samurai have wounds. Even gods have wounds.

Zatoichi had a cat, a very old cat named Shellaque. She cared for her cat with utmost tenderness. Her responsibility for the care of this cat had often stayed her hand from actions with the potential to complicate her life. Not that she was a violent woman anyway, but when inebriated a power- ful person is apt to extend herself beyond her everyday boundaries—albeit that person is inebriated on an everyday basis. It was a tribute to her great love for and sense of duty to Shellaque that even in deep intoxication, and prizing her own dignity hardly at all, Zato held herself in check.

Now it happened that Zato was a poet, not surprising given the samurai tradition of immersion in the arts visual and literary. Whether her writing was any good is not the topic here. She was a writer who cared about writing, who was nourished from it and who wished to share the records of her nourishment with others in hope of wiring through letters a network of honorable people—or at least people amenable to bringing honor into existence in the thick of an electric sea of congenitally dishonorable chumps.

What is society without connection to the individual, after all, but a massive enemy force, an occupying power in concept and in fact? And what is the individual who cannot, for whatever reason, connect to society, if not an endocolonized subject, or a de facto criminal? How does it feel to be at the mercy of a society disdainful at best? What do you suppose? Do you think it's discouraging, disenchanting and depressing? You are right. A society devolved into a loose affiliation of organs for undermining community, does not such a society necessarily self-infest with discontent? Can a society of discontents or malcontents even be called a society? A society of dissidents and dissenters is one thing, a society of discontents and malcontents is another. The latter is arguably not a society at all but a rioting prison on a runaway train.

But that's getting pretty grandiose, into mongrel metaphors, not to mention ahead of ourselves. What's important is the fact of a superhuman woman of brittle heart, poetic bent, intoxicated brain and kindly spirit, marooned within her own nation along with uncounted and unknown fellow isolated castaways. Such a woman can only sit on her tuffet for so long before the spider bites piss her off and propel her to action.

It also happened at this time that the financial sector of Zato's society had become a giant raping machine operated by laughing bankers who preserved their condition by rotating their personnel in and out of the government ostensibly responsible for regulating them, the integrity of which government suffered mightily, as you can imagine. The laughing bankers who were laughing all the day at the bank had every delusion they deserved top honors in an upside-down system. They siphoned from the productive sectors of society as much wealth as they could connive to entitle to themselves, draining away the value of actual work and injecting it into their own pockets. Magical paper financial assets ballooned in price, while payment for labor sank to the bottom of the tank.

Such relegation included all fruitful labor, from the surgeon's knife skills to the ash man's sweeping. Although children needed to be taught, farms needed tending, the ill needed treating, broken structures needed repair, polluted areas needed cleaning, the homeless needed housing, the hungry needed feeding, social phenomena needed journalizing and expressers of expression were badly in need of training, the grotesque preponderance of wealth and power was siphoned away from such necessities by the self-appointed rulers of value.

Whether our magnificent specimen of a ronin was herself possessed of poetic talent, she had amassed such a body of work and grown so deeply involved with her voice and its complex song that the desire to be read drew her in with a warping of spacetime. She felt herself plummeting toward publication as surely as a hailstone plummets from sky to Earth.

Unfortunately, her feelings were in no way reflective of fact. Publication was not a target with mass and gravity.

Publication was a process akin to distillation. Publishers chose each grain carefully and used only the purest spring water. Fermentation was a painstaking multi-step process. When the time came, the author was evaporated, with only the distillates from the vapor rendered potable. The rest of the author's self sank back into the anonymous flow of undifferentiated humanity. The process lifted the artist's power from her and diluted the rest of her, thereby disabling whatever threat even a truly great artist might pose to the status quo.

Not that anyone living or dead had or would ever have an understanding of the process as it has just been described. Such insight was certainly too subtle and enigmatic to be arrived at by anyone living at the time of the events now related. We who examine that world from outside its restrictions of imagination can see what was up. That is our luxury. That is why we can laugh at those bygone people, pity them, marvel at and revile them.

Despite the two areas of greatest individuation—one of power and one of art—the human being itself was well along in the process of dissolving. Identity had never been limited to the confines of the skin, not since humans had first become human. Identity seeped into objects and stories, symbols and machines, relationships and dreams, buildings and licenses, until by the hundred-fiftieth millennium of human development—around, perhaps, the fifth millennium of its written history proper—the center of one's identity was everywhere and its circumference nowhere. Consciousness could not be grasped by the conscious. It slipped through one's fingers and was apt to reemerge absolutely anywhere in any of infinite forms.

How was a superhero or samurai of whatever type to establish a beachhead of uniqueness in such a world of diffused identity? How was a great human beast, possessed of every kind of power with the exception of command over money and complete, unmarred, self-sufficient honor, to keep from drowning and dissolving in the oceanic and inevitable destiny of all human selves?

The money masters, of course, were fighting their own desperate war against drowning in the collective. No, if they must kill masses of millions to keep their heads above the ocean of blood, so it would be. Their seeming greed was nothing more than fear of death, but the death they feared was actually life—the life of the greater part of humanity—whereas the death Zato the superhero samurai feared and fought off with her dreams of a literary proclamation of existence was in fact death, actual and mortal.

And so Zato, being one of the hoi polloi, knew fear of real death, real death and not merely the fear of a death that is not death but relative anonymity. And somehow she came to a kind of emotional understanding of her relationships with fear and death and how they differed from the corresponding relationships among those who ruled value. And she understood the authenticity of her relationships with fear and death and the inauthenticity of those of the money-manipulating class.

So it was bound to occur to her at some point that forcing the rulers to shed their false relationships and replace them with real ones might be a worthy experiment in shaking things up and might in fact shake things up enough to loosen or even free her of the bonds binding her to an anonymity of such weight that it threatened to drown her existence altogether.

Everything is fear of death, she both reasoned consciously and sensed unconsciously. Everything is fear of death, and to alter the relationships of others to their own fears and deaths is to break ground for a new kind of social architecture, perhaps even a new kind of solid social space. Could a poet-samurai resist pursuing such a goal once its plans had been so convincingly drafted?

Zato the super samurai lived in a cave only accessible through a hidden shaft in a willow grove on the outskirts of a freight yard or via an underwater passage from the quarry itself. Hence, after ditching her Ducati and clothing and diving into the sulfurous blue water of the pit, she would swim down to the passage and along the upward incline of its submerged tunnel until she surfaced in her cave, much as a beaver enters her lodge.

It was a salt cavern. She'd draped the walls and covered the floors in carpets and carved her furniture from the very cave itself. A sea kayak, several bicycles, skis and assorted garden, kitchen and sports gear dangled here and there from a large rope net hung from the ceiling and another hung on one wall. She stole electricity to serve her meager energy needs, but that was the only thing she stole, and that only so the location of her lair might remain a secret. She did have an income: On weekend nights she worked as a sous-chef at a French-Asian fusion restaurant on Hollywood and Cahuenga called Pho-Pas.

As noted above, she had a cat. Shellaque was a calico cat, Creamsicle-orange and white, though her face and head were divided down the middle into white and black halves. She was nearly twenty years old. Zato was a sucker for living things and could not bear to see creatures abused or neglected. So when Zato received her revelation that the truth about fear and death must be communicated to those who perceived them falsely, she was unable to act on it in any way that might jeopardize her ability to care for her aging feline companion.

But one morning Zato awoke to find her very aged cat Shellaque standing very still with her forehead against a heavy chair whittled from a block of salt. The cat had gone blind in the middle of the night and within nine hours, held on Zato's lap and tended to with petting and sobbing, Shellaque had exhaled for the last time. And so the end of Shellaque's era ushered in a new and bloody chapter for the most wealthy and arrogant people on Earth. And for a certain anachronistic ronin.

As intimated, Zato was not a bloody-minded individual. Although no stranger to bitterness and even hatred, she was in no way inclined to violence as a source of amusement. This to her was an aspect of herself most precious. No realignment of another's perception of fear and death should arise from bloodlust, she reasoned. Meting out the acts of correction ought not to be enjoyable. The reward would come afterward when, in the new light of knowledge, the world was reborn and congenial. Zato assumed she would not live to see this new world but would, like Moses, send the generations into Canaan without her.

She buried Shellaque in a casket of solid salt, bought a car and drove it east. She stopped in Texas to shoot oil men in the chest. She visited several former government officials and treated them likewise. In Wyoming, she found a former vice president and shot his legs off below the knee, then hung the living man by a parachute harness from a ceiling beam in his rustic-looking living room and let his blood drain into a Le Creuset stock pot. These acts she carried out with utmost care to avoid detection, discovery and capture, as her great public act was yet to come.

In New York City, she rented a room on Broom Street. Here she prepared her manuscripts to be found. Her oeuvre comprised three volumes: one a collection of sonnets and haiku, the two others epic poems—one a memoir and the other a retelling of the *Cantar de Mio Cid* recast with animals and mythical creatures, the hero an angelic lion named Lucifer.

On a warm June night in the 151,323rd year of the human condition, Zatoichi ascended to the upper stories of a building at 60 Wall Street, climbing up the outside wall using crampons, rope and ice axes. By morning she lay in wait for those she would enlighten. Her instruments of enlightenment were two ice axes, a pair of spiky crampons for stomping on faces, a gasoline powered chainsaw, an X-Acto knife, a percussion drill and an eight-pound hickory-handled splitting maul, all of which she had carried up on her climb. I told you she was super.

She only tortured and killed those whose annual income exceeded ten million dollars, a number she'd arrived at based on a feeling. Others she merely crippled from the waist down or scarred and blinded. Clerical staff she just punched in the face unless they were a danger to the completion of her project.

Things went so smoothly that Zato feared she wouldn't be caught. In the world of these upper-echelon types, when a bloody massacre occurred, it was quarantined and ignored to prevent the spread of the very enlightenment she sought to spark. As a precaution she brought one of the executive types down in an elevator and carried him out to the streets in her arms like a baby. His hands and feet were broken—she had mashed his right hand to a stringy bleeding pulp with the flat side of the maul—and his cheeks had been punctured, half of his nose peeled off, and his left forearm drilled through. He was shrieking non-stop in a most non-human way, like a baboon being mangled in a meat grinder. A crowd gathered around Zato as she brought him to the curb, lifted him over her head and impaled his asshole on a wrought-iron fence surrounding a row of silent young elms.

Even then no one stopped her. Even then the onlookers

weren't clear a crime was being committed, let alone what it might be and who might be the perpetrator. The scene was so lurid its reality could not be attested to, and who knew what reason this woman had for doing what she'd done? And how in the hell was anyone supposed to intervene in such a spectacular assault? Zato strode, most striking and unmolested, as the impaled executive continued to gurgle his simian bleats as he drowned in his bile and blood.

Zato considered jumping in front of a bus, but she thought better of it. She had plenty of energy left, as well as the will to fight her better angels and continue her mission. She walked to another building nearby and muscled her way up to and into a very important office. The man to whom the office belonged was thrilled on first catching sight of her. She was an extremely attractive figure, even soaked in blood, her tank top clinging to her torso and breasts, thighs streaked with gore, her long hair clotted from the shoulders down, her eyes violet and furious. When she seized his throat in one bloody hand he became aroused. It wasn't until she began methodically breaking the bones of his face with the beautiful chunk of hematite he kept on his desk that he regretted misreading the drama of her appearance. The rest of his life was spent being hurled again and again at the great glass walls looking out over the city. His lungs were nearly jelly by the time Zato's efforts succeeded in sending him through the glass.

Zato lived under lockdown until her punitive death by lethal injection. Her book of short poems was published but didn't do particularly well, and neither of the two remaining volumes saw print. They became the property of a private collector, who also owned some paintings by John Wayne Gacy and Charles Manson's harmonica.

Whatever lessons she'd hoped to impart to the society from which she had lived so aloof were not learned, or, if they were, then through the miracle of self-deception they were refashioned into the wrong ones.

She did inspire a somewhat lasting work of literature, though. The poet Brenda Bede had Zatoichi in mind when writing the poem, "She Could Have Been Immortal," which first appeared in her collection *Reborn in Backgammon*:

> *Everywhere she spilled her gaze*
> *There were gardens*
> *Wrinkled ocean basins*
> *Soft Jupiters*
> *Banquets*
> *And the nations bursting into song*
>
> *She never looked into the abyss*
> *But the abyss stared out at her anyway*
> *Found a puncture point*
> *And drank the wind from her sails*
>
> *Becalmed at the center of the round horizon*
> *She and everyone else forgot her name*

Later
When the camera came to misunderstand the evidence
She was no longer on speaking terms with herself
The open window
An empty-handed gesture
Scattered her leaves across the unmade bed

AFTER BEATING A CHECHEN DRUG DEALER TO DEATH AND robbing him of the $250 he was hiding in his wing, Lao Dez Zim Ciao figured he had enough to pay five readers of his debut novel, *Lay It as It Plays*, which had already been tweeted, facebooked and youtubed in its entirety several million times. What made Ciao so sure that this time he stood on the verge of a colossal abyss of cash and adoration was that each bit that had been released teasingly and separately would be put together in an object that even his grandfather no longer called a "book."

The "book," an item of furniture cherished by the new wave of fashionistas, was widely used as interior and exterior decoration by "the rich," a notion that had also become fashionable long after the "rich" and "poor" disappeared from legal and scientific vocabularies. The street, with its ever-evolving sense of trouvée, retrouvée, re-re-retrouvée or just re-re, had revived simulated peaks and valleys of social distinction for the purpose of creating waves in the eternally placid and equal-to-itself sea of sequined neurons surfed from birth to death by genetically engineered Surfboards. In the quaint chronologies of any number of virtualities, actual paper books served as columnar details of shifting architectures; they had even been incorporated within specialized forms like Math Snails—beings engineered to function inside logics—by leaving enough room within their shells for a decorative element, such as a book. Symmetry was generally recognized as beauty: No matter how many copies replicated to create something no one could name, no singularity ever lasted longer than it took to say "singularity." Everything was named after its function (Surfboards, Math Snails, etc.) but, in a nostalgic bow to the mystery that forever refused to be mysterious, creatures gave themselves fanciful names too; an onomastics based less and less on one's actual genitors and more and more on fashion items such as books, which were admired even though no one knew how to read them.

Books had been "written" on trees in primitive alphabets that were obscure to all but Antiquaries. These Antiquaries would have been immensely "rich," if that had still mattered or if anyone would have expressed an actual interest in the contents of the books. And this is what made the Author, aka Lao Dez Zim Ciao, not only rare but also hopeful. As an Author he had the luxury or the latitude to imagine himself human; that is to say, unique. This privilege of the imagination was engineered in the entire line of Authors, each of whom imagined a different human predicament in some era of the past when humans who didn't know

they had been engineered for specific functions thought of
themselves as members of "families," "tribes," "nations" and
other such linear classifications they labored to enter into
their blogs (or books or DNA).

Lao Dez Zim Ciao had imagined a world called Detroit
in something called the twentieth century, and he had an
entire record of this place and time installed into his junk
memory. He journeyed often to Detroit to extract what in the
end would be a "novel" and, eventually, a "novel with
readers." After many visits, he created it. Then he labored,
incorrectly it turns out, to find readers by communicating
with the many beings functioning in the universe without a
specific task, engineered (unlike Surfers, let's say) to find
not-yet-named raisons d'être for their existence. (Incorrectly,
because communication is the very substance of all that
exists, and there is nothing more appropriate to the universe
than its own substance.) When Ciao realized his mistake, he
briefly considered not communicating. This wasn't possible,
so he considered miscommunicating, but this wasn't possible
either since miscommunication is still communication.
There are creatures engineered for the sole purpose of never
disbelieving; they are called angels, and they carry miscommunication back and forth with the ease of feather oil
pouring off their classical inflight forms. Communicating or
miscommunicating seemed important, though ubiquitous
and banal, to Ciao because he hadn't only written a novel;
he wanted "readers."

The only possibility for creating a "novel with readers"

was to make a "book," an object that would birth itself from a "tree," which was a protected being engineered for leafing and birds, but which was still helpless before a rare unconscious mechanism such as a "chainsaw," a mechanism that predated the virtuality Ciao lived in and could be found now and then at "virtuality auctions" where things from other universes were sold. The virtuality the chainsaw came from was called "reality," a particularly primitive world that had been purposefully engineered in "history" to contain mostly things without self-consciousness. It was this world Ciao had chosen as a setting for his "novel with readers," and it is in this world that he went shopping to set his imaginings in.

The city of Detroit had an elementary school in front of which a teenager from a "country" called Chechnya sold drugs to schoolchildren with backpacks. In "Detroit" in "history," people fashioned crudely from random discharges of the flesh, used "money" to constantly adjust their functions for the purpose of arriving at glimpses of "self-consciousness." They also used "novels" in "books" for the same reason. Lao Dez Zim Ciao reasoned, correctly this time, that in order to make his object, he had to draw from within the milieu of his creation, which is why he incorporated into a massive human who robbed and beat the Chechen drug dealer in Detroit at the end of the twentieth century in the history of a primitive universe he picked up at a street fair.

TOMORROW: **What Lao Dez Zim Ciao did with the $250 and how he found Readers** (with hints about how to pick up a "reality" at auction or even at a flea market or street fair!).

If you want to know what happened, you must buy the book. The sequel to the above will not be replicated, reproduced or even written until you, a genuine Reader, commit yourself to reading this "book."

I

"TO IMPOSE UPON ONESELF A FUTURE!" Brave words, and they reference my own sad case, which is not just my life—in view of the subject—but that of the tribe into which I was born. A tribe spawned of a riddle, really a joke, possibly a bad joke made several millennia ago, probably uttered into the neck of a clay pot as you would mutter a magical formula made to imprison a *djinn.* Such containers still existed in the wastelands of the Negev in the 1970s. The Bedouins I visited there told me of old men among their families who still knew the trick of confining *djinns* in fragile, homemade prisons, indistinguishable from a tall, bulging water-pot.

(In English, we know this apparition as a genie, the ambiguous shape shifter of the Arab sands, who cannot be called a "devil" as its inhabitants and their storytellers use the term, since a *djinn* can be good or evil, depending on its job description.)

I mention the *djinn* because usually this spirit promises some way of securing a future in this world: a magic ring or lantern as a key to untold wealth, the power to secure the hand of a princess, etc., mastery over earthly kingdoms.

The Hebrew Satan, the elder brother of the *djinn* in the literature of the West, only goes out on his Biblical trips at the express command of the Unknown. He is merely a messenger or spy for the Highest Power. He has no commission for mischief-making on his own.

As the millennia wear on, however, the storytellers of my own tribe become confused. But these are other stories, and I want to concentrate, not on tales of Satan, devils, "a band of evil angels," but on a sense of humor that follows the tribe like a malicious wind, breathing in its ears, whistling of a future.

What was the joke? Why should we talk about the amusing conundrum in the past tense, since it is still spoken and its influence has made a mockery of rational behavior for those same millennia in the Middle East?

What makes the joke so spine-tingling, good or bad, is that it imposes on its teller—the teller who takes it seriously, who is telling it about himself, herself, yourself, myself—a future, a crushing future, almost unendurable to have in one's head. And in the same breath, a moment later, it cautions, as if to posit the direct opposite, about thinking of a future at all.

Do you know when I first heard the joke?

Of course not, although if you know me at all, you could guess.

This is so abstract. You must be furious. Not only am I

withholding the joke—except for that excursion of mine among the Bedouins in my first trip to that land of the ambiguous name, Israel—but I also haven't given you a single detail.

I first heard the joke in Dorchester, Massachusetts, but whether I heard it from an adult or another child is unclear. I would hear it again and again from the age of five or six in Hebrew school, but the first whisper of it came long before I was that old.

You (the editor collecting these essays, stories, reflections), cite as your model the work of an elder statesman of literature, Jorge Luis Borges, then somewhat lightly refer to *authoterrorism*. Borges kicked me out of his house in Buenos Aires when I showed up for a visit that we had scheduled but which he had subsequently forgotten. I am being flip, much in the manner of your proposal, since distress rather than anger was the tenor of his excuse for not meeting with me. Borges was engaged with his translator when I appeared unexpectedly and barged through the front hall into his living room, forcing his maid to announce me. He offered to reschedule—but that is another story—so I cannot really claim that I was the victim of authoterrorism, although possibly I was a juvenile perpetuator. Some years later, this double of Carlos Argentino reconciled with me. We met several months before his death in a crowded room during a reception at the luxurious center for Latin American studies in one of those mansions on Park Avenue. I thought only to politely shake his hand when he grasped and drew me toward his lips. Two disciples, an older and a younger one, in the cult of the Other World, we spoke of our common influence as readers of Gershom Scholem's *Major Trends in Jewish Mysticism*. In a confidential whisper, Borges initiated me into the secrets of Kipling's sexual life. You suggest in your instructions to follow Borges in my search for authoterrorism. You define that phrase as "the madness of what lengths writers will go to promote their books in a future world where, in the literary kingdom at least, laws of decorum no longer apply, and writers will stop at nothing to get an audience."

In one of Borges' stories he writes a line that, like the iron pen of Kafka's Penal Colony that inscribes a man's sentence in his flesh, digs deeper into my chest with each passing year: "After forty, every change becomes a hateful symbol of time's passing." This is probably the key to my understanding of the future and the terror of the storyteller. (To speak of the "author" rather than the "teller" is to separate yourself from the story that tells you and allows you to hope to evade being entirely erased from the history of its narrative.)

The very idea of the future, as I read Borges, is to find the past again, to find the exact moment of the past, and to exist in it. And since it is past, only the future holds the hope that it can exist again. Still, the past is always, in some measure, a disappointment. Even those moments that were complete in themselves were succeeded by lesser moments. The dread of future extinction, which colors one's moments after the age of forty; the loss of hope for a different future; the dread that change is altering not only your body—which no longer rises at will to tumescence but now stubbornly refuses to obey your will—but alters as well the landscape around you. Buildings you admired, restaurants where you occasionally treated yourself, disappear; so do those friends whose applause you hoped to earn. You inhabit a theatre of loss, of macabre riddle at best; at worst, malignant evil.

Jesus, who crossed my path as a child, cries out in his most human chronicler, Matthew, that he has lost belief in himself. He appeals through the author for those who hear his story to believe in him. It is the most brilliant act of authorial terrorism I know, and its effects like cruel thorns were pressed by his believers into me on my splintered front steps and the concrete sidewalk below when I was four, five, six.

You must imagine me on a stone curb, above the street pavement of a peculiar concrete on Warner Street, poured as if to imitate blunt but pointed, rippling waves. It was painful, learning to ride a bike, to fall on such a surface. It guaranteed not only a skinned knee, but also a bleeding cut where you struck the street. Not a friendly asphalt surface that could be marked out in blocks with chalk for games of hopping, but a vaguely treacherous road below the sidewalk, one whose shallow hollows firmly held the drying gobs of horseshit from the junk and vegetable wagons, the milk man's van; a goblet for the flies. Here in the most elementary terms, the joke was not told, but its consequences were made clear. As a result, one was hated. In 1943, the threat was still real: Possibly, I would be murdered. A World War was raging with my life, all four years of it, the object of this conflict. (My parents, my friends, uncles, aunts, cousins, would be tossed into the furnace, but it was me they were after.) Confirmation of this came from several hoodlums a year older and younger than me, believers in a sister religion, several streets away, who ganged up on me (the Gang of Three) and beat me, giving as their reason that I had killed Jesus. Was this not the original authoterrorism? No, though I was not aware just how close this Jesus and I were at that moment.

I don't blame Jesus, or his follower Matthew, anymore.

My ancestors wrote the chronicle of the future, those first promises to Abraham, in whose tracks other dreamers followed, other religions. Borges—and I follow him—believed the future best existed in the tricky mirrors of other universes whose intervention in this we catch sight of in moments of delirium. The promises to Abraham, Isaac, Jacob, however, may have been made for this single world that Aristotle insisted was all we had to reason from, trying to understand past and future.

When we step out on the street, breathe in its air, leave the study behind, among the smells of the present it is hard not to follow Aristotle steps through a single universe.

Like Melville writing for the desk drawer—forgotten, ignored, tramping the wharves of a dying sea trade—the storyteller lapses into the author, writes his or her future down despite the discouragement of the present, commits it to "media" which is no more certain than that bottle hopelessly corked, launched with a letter upon the waves. The writer waits patiently to assume existence in the only hope of the past—the future!

Borges, poet of the mirror, as he slowly went blind and could no longer observe the inroads of the future on his image, must have seen through it. His line about the age of forty seen from the other side of the looking glass smiled back.

II

THE AUTHOR WHO THREATENS FROM THE FUTURE, and from a place in the future that holds the scales of judgment before its seat; who warns that punishment and reward will be dealt to the individual in this place and at this future time; *that* author speaking in the name of *this* future has all the instruments of fear and torture at hand. Under the guise of hope, the author abuses the present, poisons it, terrorizes us in the here and now.

Such is the anxiety of man (and woman) that institutions of great power and authority have been built on the work of such authors. Dante, whom in all other respects I love, was one of these terrorists. Merely by suggesting that he could visit such a world, he compelled the literate who followed his book after he died, as the comedy of its composition faded with the death of its contemporary readers, to imagine themselves in it as they read. The Hell he had created held them fast. He compelled them to live and die in a nightmare of belief from which he himself had escaped by a circular staircase winding up.

He did it for the sake of a Utopia, a Heaven where he could find an adolescent love and resume it. Utopia is the curse of the future imagined. The Biblical Unknown warns in the very first chapters of *Genesis* that the creation of Heaven and of utopias is the prerogative of the Holy One. Man, though, through various strategies, cannot stop dreaming of utopias if only to escape from the melancholy assurance of a final, premature extinction.

Abraham, Isaac, Jacob, all wait for instructions in their dreams. They listen. They do not command. Joseph is the first to command, but he is punished for the dream of command, and even though one of his two dreams comes true, it costs him a portion of his life. He is never lifted to the heights of his father or great-grandfather. His intimacy with the Unknown is confined to the interpretation of dreams, in particular those of others. He does not—like Jacob, Isaac, Abraham (his forefathers)—hear the Unknown speaking to him directly. He does not create a utopia for the Pharaoh in Egypt. He fashions a state of slaves, all of whom are the property of the Pharaoh, except for the priests. His brothers' children and his own children will be the victims of the very state that Joseph has brought into existence.

Moses, too, will find that to fix the dream in laws is to court punishment. When he strikes the rock to bring forth water without a previous instruction, his own utopia is taken from him. It is inevitable, though, for he is the victim of his own presumption that the future he has sketched can be brought into existence in the present.

To embark on a journey in a bathtub—that is where I have indulged myself in the minor terror that you are interested in —I have imagined the reviews I would receive. Lapped by hot water from the tap, I have assumed the persona of a reviewer, several reviewers, the ideal reader, and rewritten my career.

Why, though, seek such terror in the future? Why not the present world? I am reminded at this very moment of a young woman who proposed it to me. I met her when I was living with someone else, on the edge of breaking up, but still going back to our common apartment to sleep, eat, join bodies, both of us unwilling to face just how far we had drifted away from each other. Our attachment was strong and had gone on for six years. One day, another writer asked if I would have a cup of coffee with an English girl who had just come to Manhattan. She had no friends here. I was happy to volunteer and within minutes of meeting felt an overwhelming attraction. She responded to me in those first hours, and I found myself taking her to a friend's apartment. I discovered the sexual bliss that had been missing now for several years from my life, but slowly, the way this English girl thought about the world began to estrange me. She was also impatient with my situation, from which I could only slowly extract myself. She gave me an ultimatum. She had met someone else who had offered to move in with her. I could not break up just then, and I was growing sensitive to the differences between us. We remained friends, or so I thought. From time to time we would meet just to talk.

She had gained an editorial position on a national magazine with glossy photographs just shy of pornography but publishing fiction by writers of international reputation. I was hoping through her to place one of my stories in its pages.

She claimed to admire them but said I wasn't famous enough. To publish in her magazine, she said, I had to gain recognition.

What should I do?

"Make yourself conspicuous," she responded cheerfully, adding, when I asked how, "Murder someone."

I had lost myself in her flesh, touched a metaphysical shore, I thought. Was she angry that when I should have anchored there, I had not?

Still, her advice brings me to the place that your "authorial terrorism" does: to stop at nothing to gain an audience. Isn't that what the old rite of child sacrifice did—compelled attention? The priests had you concentrate on their story when they asked you to bring up your three-year-old to get his throat cut? Or told your daughter, a virgin, to go the night before her marriage and whore herself on the steps of their temple? The authors of those testaments knew how to make the future speak so that the city listened.

Hamburg, W. Germany, Dec. 13 *(REUTERS).*

WHILE AN ESTIMATED 150 PERSONS WAITED OUTSIDE, in the
pouring rain, for the opening of the swank new Das
Rheingeld museum in the Lebenhausen section, a series of
explosions were heard inside the museum. As the crowd
dispersed in panic, a much larger explosion occurred,
collapsing the entire building. As far as could be determined,
no injuries were sustained by the crowd—some of whom
returned to the site and picked about in the rubble, turning
up bits of plaster and fragments of oil-stained canvas, though
nothing large enough to reveal the nature or merit of the
paintings themselves. Several persons reported that the
small pieces of canvas mysteriously "disappeared" after a
short time.

Preliminary investigation failed to determine the precise
cause of the explosions, although what appeared to be wired
detonation devices were found throughout the debris.
Museum officials could not be reached for comment, nor, in

fact, could their exact identity be immediately determined, though it is presumed that they are in some way connected with the new school of painting in the Lebenhausen, the so-called "neo-Nada" group, whose work was to be exhibited publicly yesterday at the museum opening, after months of intensive advertising. Gallery owners in various parts of the city, as well as artists of other schools, were cautious in their comments as to the merit of the neo-Nada painting, which had never been shown before. "We must wait and see," was the general attitude.

ON A RECENT VISIT TO HAMBURG WE HAD OPPORTUNITY TO speak with 32-year-old Ernest Badhoff, one of the leading exponents of the new school, shortly following their ill-fated vernissage at the Rheingeld museum. The interview took place in English, and was recorded on tape. A verbatim transcript of the conversation follows:

Q: I find it curious that Hamburg should be experiencing this resurgence of advanced creativity.

Herr Badhoff: Nothing could be more logical. Germany is a nation of philosophers and art, after all, is merely an extension of philosophy—a clever or attractive way of making a philosophic statement. My God, what a sense of realism it has brought! A strange new kind of realism—an almost imaginative realism, you might say.

Q: I see. Well, now about your work—the work of the neo-Nada group—how many are you?

Herr Badhoff: I am not at liberty to divulge that. I can tell you this much, our vernissage featured the work of twelve painters.

Q: You mean the October 1st show at the Rheingeld?

Herr Badhoff: Yes. I had seven paintings in the show, the others about the same. In all, there were 85 paintings in the show.

Q: Well, perhaps I'm mistaken, but I was given to understand that your work—the work of your group—has not yet been shown publicly nor, in fact, has it been seen by anyone I've been able to meet.

Herr Badhoff: You see, ideally a painting—or any other work of art, for that matter— occurs, both in conception and execution, solely in the mind of the artist. Only persons unsure of their conceptions, and lacking any inner sense of form and color, find it necessary to bring the painting into material existence. Such persons, of course, have no real or noteworthy connection with contemporary art.

Q: I see. Well, now I understand there is an American here who is quite prominent in your group.

Herr Badhoff: That is correct. Jack Dandy he is called—he was here during the war, as a soldier, and deserted from the U.S. Army. As you may know, he is a quadruple amputee, one of very few.

Q: I see. Well, how does he manage to paint with this… this very serious handicap?

Herr Badhoff: All I can say is he literally throws himself into his canvas.

Q: But you have never actually seen his work, have you?

Herr Badhoff: Again correct. No one has seen his work. We do not show our work, not to anyone.

Q: Now your vernissage at the Rheingeld was spoiled, wasn't it–by the explosions, I mean. How did that happen?

Herr Badhoff: No, no, that was the vernissage.

Q: The work, the paintings, deliberately destroyed?

Herr Badhoff: No, no, that isn't the point. You have to see the totality of it. The paintings did not exist at the time of the explosions. Those paintings were done with an oil-based pigment, you understand, tinctured with acid–sulphuric acid, six-percent solution–giving them a physical duration of about 72 hours. The paintings were non-existent before the explosions.

Q: Well, now just what was the point?

Herr Badhoff: The point? What point?

Q: Well, of the whole thing.

Herr Badhoff: Ah yes, that was the point–the "whole thing!" Yes, that was the point precisely!

Q: But at the time you were hanging your pictures for the show, you must have seen some of the other work then.

Herr Badhoff: Ah ha! No, I did not! We did not see each others' work at that time. Each canvas was covered with a loose drape which had been treated with a seventy-percent acid solution. This drape dissolved in about two hours–by which time we were all out of the building. But–and this might interest you–for perhaps six hours, there were 85 marvelous, never before seen, pictures there on exhibition, in a totally empty museum!

Q: And then…

Herr Badhoff: Ka-blooie! Nada!

Q: It is difficult to understand how patronage can occur if there are no paintings to be seen or purchased.

Herr Badhoff: Well, you must realize that as an art evolves, so does its patronage. Patrons come to expect quite different things from what they expected in the past.

Q: And just what do you give your patrons in exchange for their support?

Herr Badhoff: What any art gives its patrons—the privilege of identifying with the latest and greatest.

Q: May I ask if there were any dissentions, for example, to the plan of destroying the museum?

Herr Badhoff: Yes, Jack Dandy wanted the museum filled with people, taking their last earthly look… at non-existent paintings! Then ka-blooie! Nada!

Q: Well, that's quite an idea–. Still, I hope I never get into one of your showings by mistake, ha, ha.

The Grip of Love /

"OTHERS HAVE BOMBS OR KNIVES OR GUNS. Others have poisons. All I have are words. Words are all I have. I can move them around in my mind or on the page, but they are the only weapons I possess." I wrote that paragraph for my first novel. At the time I was not aware of the irony.

Irony? Dishonesty. I have had other weapons. I have been in possession of several household poisons. I have owned knives. Once I had a gun. I bought it when I was married to my first wife, Louise, because I needed power in that marriage, power of any kind, and a gun seemed like a start. It was an old pawn shop pistol, and I never really knew how to use it. I'm sure that Louise never saw it and not sure if she even knew I had it. It sat in a shoebox high up in the closet. Eventually, the box acquired cobwebs along one side. Then, long after I left Louise, the gun came back into the picture. I shot a doorframe while trying to shoot a man.

Trying? Failing. I shot a doorframe, much to the displeasure of my second wife, Fay. Fay has hair that is as black as the feathers of a raven. It is not her best feature. I can't speak to that without descending into pornography. It is not her worst feature, either. Her worst feature is her temper, and the way her eyes narrow brightly when she submits to that temper. "I am not getting in that car until you promise me that you'll finish what you started," she might say. "I won't let you give up. I don't like quitters. Promise me, or I am going to stand here and stare a hole right through your goddamned window."

She might say? She said. It was nearly two years ago, in the fall, when we moved together from Chicago to New Orleans. The car was black, though not as black as her hair. The sun was bright, though not as bright as her eyes. I eventually promised, and Fay settled down and got into the car and turned on the radio and kissed me on the shoulder by way of apology. Off we went, north to south, hopelessness to hope, some rockabilly on the radio to reinforce the point. Rockabilly? Well, it was country music, hopped up to high speeds, with a touch of pedal steel. It wasn't exactly rockabilly. But it had the same feel, and when I have told this story previously, I have mostly said that it was rockabilly, so for all intents and purposes, it was.

FAY HAD PRIED ME OUT OF MY MARRIAGE TO LOUISE, and, once out, I knew I couldn't stay in Chicago. "Cities are lovers, in a sense," I have said in interviews. "They are held and they are watched carefully and then, sometimes, they are left." Fay and I left. Over the telephone, mostly, we bought an old house in the French Quarter. There were shabby parts in the pictures, and I promised her that I'd get to work on the sidewall and the backyard, but we both knew there was no chance of that. I was 32-years-old and was well into final revisions on my first novel, *Jonah and Me*. At the time, the book had consumed me for the better part of a year, which was roughly the same amount of time that I had been with Fay. This may be difficult to believe, given the fame that it has since achieved, but I had no real confidence that I could bring it into focus, let alone finish it. That is what Fay meant when she said "quitters," and it's what I meant when I promised her I would not become one. The process of focusing and finishing required substantial changes, not only to the title (there is a reason it is unfamiliar: it was never used) but to the first chapter and the second and much of the third, as well as to the names of two of the three principal characters and to the setting and to the overall theme. "True revision makes relentless and unforgiving demands," I have said in interviews. "It is the author's version of time itself." I meant it the first time I said it. By now it is just something to say, as empty and essentially untrue as the remark about how words are an author's only weapon.

Back then, in the car, driving from Chicago to New Orleans, with rockabilly on the radio and the manuscript of *Jonah and Me* in the trunk, I had not yet begun to give interviews for the novel, and so I did not have a repertoire of prepared statements. I was not yet confident enough of anything to say it once, let alone repeatedly. At the time, I drove, and Fay sat beside me, and I thought mostly about the first chapter, which loomed large in my mind, especially the first sentence. "I was a little messed up when I drove my car through the county fair." The chapter went on to detail the financial, romantic and psychological troubles of my loosely autobiographical protagonist, James Pentilla, a man in the world feeling no power, only pain, and wondering how he could treat the latter and aspire, however imperfectly, to the former. James was feeling murderous toward Howard Alter, the former lover of his new wife, who was also the owner of a small television station in the fictional city of Barrier, Illinois. Howard Alter was making money and holding it high as he made it clear that he was coming back for Georgina, James Pentilla's new wife, who was the daughter of a local lumber magnate and so had money of her own, a fact that both left her immune to Howard Alter's wealth and attracted her to it, birds-of-a-feather style. If these details are confusing, so be it. It is not important to keep track of them. They belong to *Jonah and Me*, a novel that, in turn, is located on an alternate fork in the road of my life. It is not the novel that came to be. It is a novel that came to not be. I am the only one who ever read the original draft of the novel in its entirety, and so it exists only within me, in my memory. "True revision, like time, is irreversible," I have said in interviews.

At the time, as I have said, I was done with the novel, but also not nearly done. The middle had been worked on and worked over but it was still far from fit: there were so many issues with it, imprecisions in the description of James Pentilla's kind but limited face, loose joints in the handling of Georgina's accent and her more disreputable predilections, clouds in the motives of Howard Alter. "I can't wait to get to New Orleans," I said to Fay. "A new place, a new lease. I'll be writing like a fiend the minute I go through the door." She was nearly asleep but she murmured in assent.

ONE WEEK LATER I HAD NOT ADDED OR SUBTRACTED A WORD. Fay and I had bought furniture from a swap meet, put our clothes into dressers, flopped a new mattress on an old platform bed, and christened it with four days of lovemaking. I credit Fay with both the idea and the successful execution of it, in the sense that she extracted from me the excitement of a full collaborator. With my first wife, Louise, I had been uninterested in sex, in part because she was too interested in a way I found off-putting: We were always trying to have a child, never succeeding, which only fired her resolve. Louise was on me like a drill sergeant on a new recruit, and she had no compunction about telling me exactly where to put my hands or my mouth. I should add that I was, for most of my marriage to Louise, roughly 100 pounds overweight. I had glasses whose frames bowed outward as a result of the massive circumference of my head. So picture the scene (or, if it repulses you, do not): the athletic, driven Louise, compact and blonde, clambering aboard a tired, defeated dirigible of a husband and inflating him, without mercy, to the point of bursting.

No, not a dirigible. The metaphor is inelegant and possibly nonsensical. Say instead: Louise riding a whale while standing up and feeling a sense of accomplishment, never any fear or wonder, when the great creature spouted through its blubber-lined blowhole. That is a more apt image, because it is the one I had in my mind whenever Louise and I were engaged in the act. She was a whaler, and she had leapt from the safety of her boat to the back of the leviathan. I was punctured by harpoons. I was subdued by the ferocity of the smaller being. I was brought in for ambergris and ivory. I wish that I had been more than that to her, but I never was: She never had an extended conversation with me, never asked after my writing, never told me what she was feeling. She wanted a baby so definitively that her desire crowded all else out of the picture. To twist the metaphor in on itself, she wanted the baby like Ahab wanted the white whale, which was me, and as a result she did not really want me at all. It was that sense of myself that gave me the title for my first published short story, "He Swims Away," and—now that I think of it—the original title of my novel as well. Every morning that Louise went off to work, I hoped it would be the last time I would see her. The fact that I spent half of each morning feeling guilty about that wish did not make it any less true.

When I met Fay, I was sitting in a coffee shop, writing. She walked by, noticed what I was doing, continued walking. Due to the positioning of the table and shelves she saw only my head and shoulders, and only for a second. She came back over a few minutes later and said that she had read a single sentence walking by, but that it struck her as a good sentence and possibly a great one. She was wearing a tight black sweater and her hair was pulled tightly behind her head. She was beautiful. Hearing that a new, unknown, beautiful woman liked my writing was enough for me. I stood. She gasped and held on to a chair so as not to fall. "There was so much of you," she said later. "I just wanted to take your hand and tell you that I was going to improve you. Addition by subtraction." In fact, she asked me to dinner. I told her I was married. She said she didn't care. "She's not invited," she said. Three weeks later, I told Louise that I was unhappy. She suggested that a baby might help. A day after that, I told her that I was in love with someone else.

Almost immediately after I moved out of the little house I shared with Louise and into an apartment with Fay, I began to lose weight. The reason was Fay's regimen, which was simple and effective. She changed my diet. She forced me to exercise. And she played hard to get, which in turn made me want to go and get her, at which point she was happily, acrobatically gotten. Within six months, I had lost fifty pounds. Within eight months, I had lost 65. All of this was made possible by the loss of the first hundred and 25: Louise, I mean. She and I never had a child, but now I had one of my own: "Jonah and Me," born from my discontent with Louise, nursed by Fay's focused and acrobatic ardor. I did not let Fay read the manuscript, but I dedicated it to her. "The ink in the book will be the color of your hair," I said.

"Think of it as a tribute."

One day, Fay came home from work—she was an assistant to a lawyer—and told me that we were moving to New Orleans. I asked why. "Because you are done here," she said. "I see it in your expression. I hear it in your voice. There's no more inspiration for you in this place. And you are always talking about New Orleans."

"I had thought about setting a small section there," I said. "But I thought we would just take a vacation."

"No," she said. "We'll move. I found us some houses as possibilities. I want it to be a success, just like I want you to be a success." Her tone was unmistakable. She meant it. The night before we moved, she explained to me that she was proud that I had lost so much weight, because it would permit her to protect me. She explained further: Louise had wanted to take something from me and had fattened me for that purpose. Fay wanted to carry me along with her, and so she needed me lean. "I can carry you along with me," I said. She smiled but said nothing.

So we drove down from Chicago and arrived in New Orleans, and Fay and I fornicated for four days. We were on the bed and next to it, in the bathtub and up against the closet door. On the fifth day, I stayed her with what I thought was a valid excuse. "I need to work," I said. She began to narrow her eyes. "No, no," I said. "None of that. You know why we came here. Chicago got me to Level A. But we came here because you said that with a new location and new pressures, I could write something that would take me to

Level B, if not C or D."

"I'm not complaining," she said. "I am just surprised that you have the wherewithal. Proud. Get to it."

I got to it. I went into my office and began to write. "I'm going out," Fay called from the other room. I grunted an answer.

I worked mostly on the middle. It was the middle that needed the most work. In that sense, my novel and I were one. I refined what I knew of James Pentilla. I gave Georgina fuller lips. Howard Alter grew monstrous and then meek, and I decided to let him have both: clouds as shades of gray. Every day I worked. Every day Fay went out. By degrees I crept closer to completion, and then, after about three weeks, I was done. I notified Fay by reaching for her at night, in bed, a privilege I had not been allowed until the book was finished. "That's news," she said.

The next day, we celebrated as we had when we first arrived in New Orleans: acrobatics, with some alcohol added in for good measure. I slept from afternoon to evening, woke, went back to bed with Fay, drank more, and then went out like a light until the morning. All in all, it was the behavior of a king.

"You know," Fay said the next day. "Don't you always say that after a book is done, then the author has to truly finish it?"

"Sure," I said. "I believe that."

"Do you want to take one more day just to touch things up?"

"I guess."

"Like that aquarium scene."

"The aquarium scene?"

"In that it? The one you mentioned last night."

"I did?"

"Sure. You said that you thought that it went too slow."

"I don't remember saying that. Though it's true. I could put some polish on it."

"To be the best," she said. "In the meantime, let's put the manuscript in the drawer with the jewelry and the other valuables. That's where it belongs." She picked it up and carried it across the room. Then she came back and kissed me on the cheek. "This is what we've been working toward for more than a year," she said. "Can I give you one more before you get back to it?"

Fay went out in the morning like usual. I got to the aquarium scene. James was standing with Howard Alter in front of a tank of rays. Each was holding a picture of Georgina. I pruned, trimmed, tried to streamline. An hour passed, maybe a little less, when I heard something clatter to the ground just outside the north wall of the house. I went to the window and looked out. There was a slim man crouched by the bushes, wearing black pants, a maroon sweater and a stocking pulled entirely over his head. He was holding a small silver pistol. I stepped away from the window before the man could see me, but in my haste, I knocked against the desk. A cup filled with pencils fell to the floor. The man's head turned up at me quickly, like that of a bird. Then he came out of his crouch and walked toward the front door.

I was panicked. I hurried to the desk, where I kept my ancient pistol, and dug it out from behind papers and pens. It was lighter in my hand than I expected, and colder to the touch. The man was already fiddling with the doorknob. It was not locked. Fay never locked it. I hid my gun behind my back.

The man shoved the door open. He came inside. "Stop," I said. He did not stop, though he did not advance. He raised his gun and pointed it at me. "What do you want?" He motioned toward the kitchen and tilted his head, again with the birdlike motion. "You want me to go in the kitchen? Why? So you can rob me?" He nodded. I took a step as if I meant to comply, then produced the pistol from behind my back and pulled the trigger. It missed him wide left and splintered the frame of the door.

"Damn it," the man said. He lowered his gun and pulled off his mask. It was not a man. It was Fay. "You don't know how to use that thing. You could have hurt me. Give it to me." I handed her the gun.

"What?" I said. I was good only for the single word and then I sunk back into mute relief.

Fay stared at me. Her eyes narrowed and then widened again. She took off her sweater and unbound her breasts. She sat on the edge of the bed. "Come over here," she said. "Let's do it while it's still exciting. Then I'll explain."

She was right, and I knew it, and I went over to her. Afterwards, I worked up the courage to ask her again. "So why did you come back into our house with a gun?"

She sighed and closed her eyes for a long time. When she spoke, they were still closed. "I was coming to steal your manuscript."

"Why?"

"This is hard for me to say," she said. "I read it. It's terrible."

"You read it? When?"

"Yesterday, when you were passed out. That's how I knew about the aquarium scene. But that's the least of your problems. The whole thing is...well, let me show you." She stood up and, still naked, took the small silver pistol in her hand and shot right through the center of the title page. "I was going to take this manuscript and put it somewhere safe. Like the bottom of a river. You would have just assumed the thief grabbed it while he was getting the jewelry."

"That's why you made me put it with the other valuables?" I said.

"Shh," she said. "Let me think."

THREE DAYS PASSED WITHOUT SEX OR CONVERSATION. We didn't eat meals together, and when I ate alone, I ate like I did when I was with Louise. I gained four pounds quickly, like I had taken it down from a shelf. Now and then I went back to the manuscript, but now I saw it as Fay did, and there was no point to any of it. The night of the third day, Fay sat down next to me and took my hand. "I have an idea," she said.

"Okay."

"Shoot me."

I squinted. That was how my eyes narrowed: from confusion.

"I'm serious," she said. "I don't know why I didn't think of it in the first place. You know that scene where James accidentally stabs Georgina? Well, change it to shooting. He can get the gun from the guy who owns the bar next to Howard Alter's car lot. Maybe that guy thinks that James is going to use it against Howard. Whatever. You're the writer. Anyway, James shoots Georgina in the leg."

"Okay," I said. "And what does this have to do with you?"

"Everything," she said. "If the book has a shooting, I'll get shot so that it's partly real. That gives it legitimacy."

"I refuse," I said. "I would never hurt you."

"It won't hurt," she said. "I'll load up on painkillers. I'll drink. We'll make sure we have all the first aid we need. We'll look up exactly where it's safe to be shot. I think the back of the leg, just above the knee, isn't so bad. Then I'll call the emergency room. They'll probably notify the police. They probably have to. But I won't press charges. I'll say we were getting a little rowdy, or that I had given you cause." She was speeding through the course now. "We'll work that out. The point is that you shoot me and we have a record of it so that when the book comes out, there's a real story behind it."

"When the book comes out?" I brightened. "So you think it's good enough to be published?"

"Hardly," she said. "But this will push it across. The lawyer I worked for sometimes represented authors, so I have a sense of that. When you put memoir in your fiction, it moves it farther on down the road."

We prepared. Or rather, Fay prepared. She was meticulous as in all things. She laid out the bandages. She put a tape mark on the ground next to the kitchen table where she wanted me to stand. She put rockabilly on the radio—"for ambiance," she said. She marked the spot on her leg with a dollop of shaving cream. Then she stood by the couch and I took my derelict old pistol, and I shot her in the leg. I can't swear to it but I am fairly certain that before she screamed in pain she smiled.

"A PIE GOES ON THE TABLE, a pie goes in the face. Context is everything." That is the first line from the first review of *Grip*. It went on to praise the book as "a blackly comic refraction of a very real trauma, with an awkwardness that seems to come from its uneasy relationship with what we commonly think of as 'real life.' The question of its reality was addressed at length: "Most readers are no doubt familiar with the celebrated case of the author, who shot his second wife during an argument, and who then, to the disbelief of nearly everyone, reconciled with her only three months later. 'His talent had costs,' she said famously, 'but more than that, it had value.' The two of them—author and subject, artist and muse, perpetrator and victim—stand at the crossroads of a particular kind of modern fame. The swiftness of the bullet illustrates the speed of modern communication, and the speed with which modern judgment dissipates. It is impossible to say if this novel would be a success, or even an entity, without the facts that underlie it. It is also unnecessary to say."

The novel—which was still dedicated to Fay, though with a much simpler "I'm sorry"—has remained at or near the top of the best-seller list for more than half a year. Fay and I live in a large house about eight blocks from the little one with the crumbling north wall. As a result of my celebrity and the benefits that accompany it, I have put on about forty pounds. Fay is losing interest in me, a bit, and she thinks she wants a baby. "I am lucky that the shot only hit me mid-thigh," she says in interviews, laying a hand on herself to illustrate. "Lower down and it could have been curtains for certain." She meant it the first time she said it. By now it is just something to say.

Author Bios

WHITNEY ANNE TRETTIEN is working toward a PhD in English at Duke University. She has created, produced and/or published on seventeenth-century generative writing, moving parts in books, fore-edge paintings, digital poetry, bibliobotanies and early modern plant-animal hybrids. Visit her online at whitneyannetrettien.com.

NILE SOUTHERN is a writer and filmmaker, originally from New York City, living with his wife and two children in Boulder, Colorado. He is also the Trustee of the Terry Southern Literary Trust. Nile's book *The Candy Men: The Rollicking Life and Times of the Notorious Novel, Candy* (Arcade), won 'Book of the Year' for Creative Non-Fiction in Colorado. Nile also co-edited *Now Dig This: The Unspeakable Writings of Terry Southern 1950-1995* (2000, Grove). He has written magazine articles for STOPSMILING, *Filmmaker*, and *The National Herald*. His fiction has appeared in *O-Blek*, *Open City*, *Black Ice (FC2)*, and *The Paris Review*. His e-book, *The Anarchists of Eco-Dub: A Novel of Convergence* is distributed by the literary website altx.com. He has recently written "Greeks Out West," a documentary radio series funded in part by the Colorado Endowment for the Humanities. His work in film has appeared at the Whitney Biennial as part of Mark Amerika's installation Grammatron, and at such venues as the Theatre for the New City and La Mama. His current project is *Dad Strangelove*, a film about the life and legacy of his father, Terry Southern.

DAVID REES is a freelance wine consultant and budding fashion-industry insider who lives on the cutting edge of innovation and style. You can usually find him at the hottest club or the trendiest new restaurant.

JEFFREY DORCHEN was born in Detroit, Michigan. He is a writer, actor, musician, artist and radio pundit. A founding member of the internationally acclaimed Chicago-based Theater Oobleck, his award-winning, innovative perfor-mance and theater work has been produced to critical acclaim in New York City, Chicago, Los Angeles and South Africa and garnered him a MacArthur Foundation grant. He is a nationally published essayist who for the past thirteen years has delivered political commentary on the weekly public affairs show This Is Hell, (WNUR, Evanston and Chicago). He has also appeared on several episodes of public radio's This American Life. His one-act play "Ubu Papa" appears in the current issue of *The Louisville Review*. He is working on a book about the parallels between iconography

depicting the Hindu god Ganesh and the Jewish lay and
religious exegetical traditions. He lives in Los Angeles.

ANDREI CODRESCU (codrescu.com) was born in Sibiu,
Transylvania, Romania. His first book was *License to Carry a
Gun* (1970), and his most recent are *The Posthuman Dada Guide:
Tzara and Lenin Play Chess*, (2009) *The Poetry Lesson* (2010) and
*Whatever Gets You through the Night: A Story of Sheherezade and the
Arabian Entertainments* (2011). Codrescu founded *Exquisite
Corpse: a Journal of Books & Ideas, 1983–2011* (corpse.org), and
taught literature and poetry at Johns Hopkins University,
University of Baltimore, and Louisiana State University. In
1989 he covered the fall of the Ceausescu regime for NPR
and ABC News, and wrote "The Hole in the Flag: an Exile's
Story of Return and Revolution." He is a regular commenta-
tor on NPR's All Things Considered, and has received a
Peabody Award for the film *Road Scholar.*

MARK JAY MIRSKY is the editor of *Fiction*, a magazine he
co-founded with Donald Barthelme, Max Frisch and Jane
deLynn. A professor of English at the City College of New
York he has published four novels: *Thou Worm Jacob, Blue Hill
Avenue* (recently listed by the Boston Sunday Globe as one of
the 100 essential books about New England) *Proceedings of the
Rabble, The Red Adam*, and a collection of novellas, *The Secret
Table.* Other books of his include *My Search for the Messiah,
Dante, Eros and Kabbalah, The Absent Shakespeare*, and the
forthcoming *The Drama in Shakespeare's Sonnets: "A Satire to*

Decay." He is the editor of the *Diaries of Robert Musil* in English, and has co-edited the collection *Rabbinic Fantasies* and a historical volume, *The Jews of Pinsk, 1506-1880.* His play "Mother Hubbard's Cupboard" was produced at Manhattan's Fringe Festival in 2007.

TERRY SOUTHERN (1924–1995) was an influential writer known for his unique, comic voice. His novels include *Flash and Filigree, Candy, The Magic Christian, Blue Movie* and *Texas Summer.* His short stories have been anthologized in the collections *Red Dirt Marijuana and Other Tastes* and *Now Dig This: The Unspeakable Writings of Terry Southern,* edited by Nile Southern and Josh Alan Friedman. Gore Vidal called him "the most profoundly witty writer of his generation," while Norman Mailer called him the "heir to Nathaniel West." In the early 1950s in Paris, Terry was part of *The Paris Review* crowd and also published with Maurice Girodias (*Candy*) and Girodias's *Olympia Review* in which Herr Badoff appeared. His biting satirical wit displayed in *Dr. Strangelove* and *Easy Rider* (both recipients of Academy Award Nominations for Best Screenplay) continues to influence generations of writers and directors. His film credits include *Barbarella, The Loved One, The Cincinnati Kid, End of the Road* and *The Telephone.* Tom Wolfe credits Terry's "Twirling at Ole Miss" story, published in *Esquire,* as the first instance of the "New Journalism" phenomenon made popular by Hunter S. Thompson. His e-books are available through Open Road Media (openroadmedia.com).

BEN GREENMAN is an editor at *The New Yorker* and the author of several acclaimed books of fiction including *Superbad*, *Please Step Back*, and *What He's Poised To Do*. His most recent book is *Celebrity Chekhov*. He lives in Brooklyn.